www.gravymedia.com

ISBN: 978-1-9164216-9-1

A CIP catalogue record for this book is available from the British Library.

First published by Boz Publications Ltd 2020

Boz Publications Ltd.

71-75 Shelton Street, Covent Garden, London WC2H 9JQ

office@bozpublications.com - www.bozpublications.com

OH! LOOK! A FOX!

CONNOR'S GUIDE TO TAMING ADHD

NATHAN ERASMUS

MONIKA DZIKOWICZ

This book is dedicated to everyone struggling with taming their fox.

FROM NATHAN

To my parents, thanks for giving me space to be myself whilst growing up.

To Nollaig McSweeney and Andy Smithyman,
thanks for all your support in the development stages.

Thanks to Sarah Erasmus for all your amazing editing skills,
and Isabel Hulf for your awesome proofreading.

For my kids, Eloise and Enzo, thank you for helping me rediscover my inner child.
No words can express how much I love you both.

To my wife, Livia: it seems you've married a Manchild!
Thank you for supporting my ideas, hustle and playful parenting.
You will always be my perfect partner and a wonderful mother.

FROM MONIKA

Thanks to Krzysztof Skorb for unbroken belief,
and to Kenny Vallenca for your keen eye.

Connor's a creative boy
with many dreams and thoughts.

He wants to be a Youtuber,

a Ninja,

or an Astronaut.

Even though all of these jobs may seem extremely cool,
right now he must stop daydreaming and quickly get to school.

On Monday morning teacher
clearly writes out the day's tasks,
but Connor isn't watching,
instead he's designing masks.

A new idea distracts him, his attention goes elsewhere...
"Create an animation!" whilst the teacher's unaware.
He carefully draws stickmen in the corners of his pages,
when finished it looks awesome, but it's taken blimming ages!
He sadly can't remember anything his teacher taught,
this often seems to happen at the times that he gets bored.

After school, his mum asks him to go and buy bread,
but he forgets because he's crafting rhymes inside his head.

Next day Miss Feta asks them to present their work to class.
Poor Connor starts to panic, and is desperate to go last.
When everyone has had their turn and he is the last one,
he nervously walks to the front, not wanting to look dumb...

To try and hide his lack of work he tells some jokes instead!
The kids are in hysterics but the teacher's face goes red!
Miss Feta, she is fuming as she yells at him: *"SIT DOWN!"*
Connor's in her bad books and is now the new class clown.

Today is now a new day and Connor knows the rule:

Ignore ADDam the fox so he can do better at school.

He gets to class so early, he arrives before the bell.

It's hard to pay attention but he manages quite well.

"I'm tired, I don't want to hear about this imaginary fox!
I suggest tomorrow, if you don't want to be grounded, you pull up your socks!"

And just when Connor thinks that it's the end of all the gloom,
his mum reminds him he still needs to tidy up his room.
"Tidying is boring! I like fun and want to play!"
But now's no time for tantrums, Connor won't get his own way.
He gets sent to his bedroom without having any supper.
All teary-eyed he's hoping that tomorrow will be better.

"Mom! I want to sit still and I can be a good guy,

I just don't find it easy but I try, I really try.

I want to work hard like you do, work harder than an ox,

it's just I get distracted by Addam the naughty fox!

He drives my thoughts towards the things that always look like fun,

I just can't stop to think how it may look to everyone.

And when I realise inside exactly what he's done,

it's too late to do better...and my chance to change has gone."

When he gets home his mum looks cross,
as Connor boasts of fun in class.
"Well, I've heard from your teacher, son,
that you've been acting like an ass!"
"What?!
Like a bottom!
That's
sooo funny!"

"Connor!
Don't be cheeky with me!
'Ass' means a donkey or a mule.
You've been disrupting kids in school
and acting like a fool."

Breaktime comes, and Connor runs - he loves to play football.
The problem is he hogs it and won't pass the ball at all!

Sometimes when he gets excited, he forgets to share.
And when it comes to tackling rough he doesn't seem to care.

He comes across too hyper,
on the pitch - a tearaway.
So Connor's mates from school
suggest another game to play.

It's really their excuse
to leave him hurt, and get away.
The hurt then turns into anger
and he throws a rage grenade.

He loses self-control:
as a result, kicks off real bad.
And whilst overreacting,
goes and boots his own comrade!

**Although on the outside
it seems he's really mad,
inside he wants to fit in
and is feeling really sad.**

But Miss Feta has been sitting by the window spying.
She storms onto the playground, whilst the other child is crying.

*"Connor! I saw everything! I'm writing to your mum
tomorrow after school you must stay late for detention!
This kind of bad behaviour, it deserves a suspension!
It's time I bring your actions to your mother's attention!"*

When Connor reaches home that night he gives the note to mum.
He tries hard to explain himself. The damage though, is done.
Mum reads the note and instantly, is angry and upset.
They argue first, then Connor goes to bed, his eyes all wet.

Thursday morning comes around, it's time to do group work,

but after Connor's tantrum, most kids think that he's a jerk.

Even though he's funny they've seen he can go berserk...

Which means he gets picked last,
behind class bully Murky Dirk...

They need to pick a group leader and Connor calls 'shotgun',
but gets himself into a mess before he has begun.
He's having trouble leading his team's organisation.
The whole day starts to feel full of humiliation.
His team all fear his actions since he kicked Dan in the bum.
Soon Connor realises that today won't be much fun.

Later when the day ends and the progress has been slow,
Connor's team have struggled as they could not find their flow.
The other teams have finished scripts - and they're all good to go.
Tomorrow they must all perform their work at the school's show.

All the other kids leave school at regular home time,
but Connor has detention and must write 200 lines...

His actions mean the team
isn't ready for the pantomime.
And what is worse his mum arrives
to talk through all his 'crimes'.

Miss Feta comes to greet his mum,
her face is beetroot red.
Connor tries his best to eavesdrop
all the things now said.
A lot he can't make out
although he hears teacher suggest:

***"STRONG MEDICATION
SHOULD CALM HIM DOWN,
I NOW THINK
THAT'S WHAT'S BEST!"***

His mum remains completely calm,
as she responds with folded arms:

***"I think your recommended
drugs are too strong for my kid,
and numbing personalities
is not my way to live.***
*What about more exercise
and also movement breaks,
I'm totally supportive
of whatever it might take.
Managing his diet well
should calm him down,
'less wired'
but I can't guarantee
that this will ever
make him quiet".*

When they get home later, Connor cuddles up to mum.
She doesn't feel so tired, so is more patient with her son.

"I thought about our talk, sweetheart. About Addam your friend.
I don't know much about him but I want to understand.

Addam seems to love art and I know he's here to stay.
Once others understand him more they can help you behave.

The fox adds to your character and gives you creativity,
he just requires more care to manage his hyperactivity.

I was thinking we should spell his name a little differently.
Attention-deficit is no disorder so remove one 'D'?

With regular sleep and good healthy food,
the fox won't take over in making you rude.
It's possible to learn how you can make your red friend tame,
so he will not get in the way from you raising your game.

Using creativity will help him be more meek.
And make friends with your fox because
HE MAKES YOU SO UNIQUE."

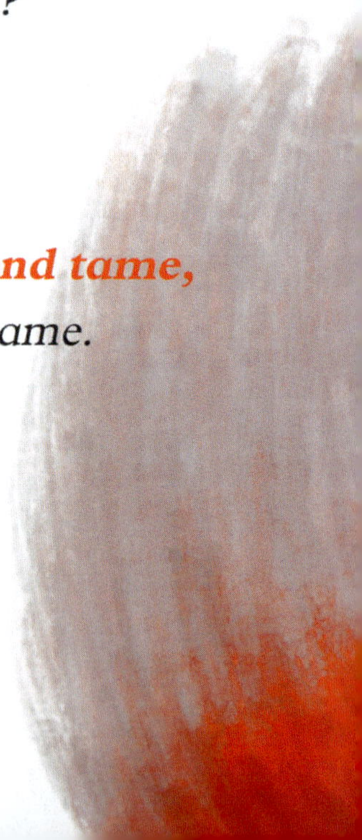

As Connor goes to bed that night and gets under his quilt,
he thinks about his week and he is riddled full of guilt.
The one thing though he realises now, at the day's end;
His mother understands him and is also his best friend.

Friday finally arrives, the pantomime's today.
Connor's group is unprepared,
it feels more like doomsday!
As Connor's nowhere to be found they have no play to show.
His teammates ask to join another group,
morale is very low.

But then appearing at the door
comes Connor with a smile:
"Guys! Here's our script, don't worry!
I've been writing all this while. We're ready to present!
I've been creating through the night.
I didn't want to let you down!"
His team cheer with delight.

Connor's creativity
was focused on the task.
So dedicated to his team,
his talent shines at last.

Unlike the other kids' plays, that were all super cliché,
Connor's made amazing masks out of paper maché.
His script is fun and honest and its meaning is immense,
explaining life with Adam - his perspective now makes sense.

Jj
Kk
Ll
Mm
Nn
Oo
Pp

Connor's mum is watching,
she feels happy and so proud.
Her son's play was not only fun,
but also quite profound.

The audience all clap
as it's the ending of the play.
His group all bow and hug.
The audience all cheer:
"HOORAY!"

Despite the last few days that felt like they had sprung from hell,
his friends now all forgive him and they understand him well.
Connor has bounced back and he has turned from foe to chum,
all thanks to understanding friends and help from his great mum.
The way this week has turned around was all quite unexpected,
though Connor's just relieved to feel he's finally been accepted.

BEST YOUTUBER
1000000000000 SUBSCRIBERS
KARATE NINJA MASTER
MUM
MY AWARD FOR BEST PANTOMIME
ME
OLIVIA IS THE FUNNIEST EVER!!!
JOY IS SO SMART!
MY FRIEND
JAKE IS COOL!

HA HA HA
HA HA
I AM SORRY I KICKED YOU.
DAN
MOM SAID BUTT! HA HA HA
HA HA HA
I SAID SORRY TO DAN HE SAID IT IS OK AND WE WILL STILL BE FRIENDS.
MRS FETA SAID MY SHOW WAS AMAZING AND I AM TALENTED!
MRS. FETA
THE END